Glee
Club

Glee Club

JO COTTERILL

With illustrations by
Jen Collins

Barrington Stoke

For Phoebe Haywood,
who chose the name Melody Gold

First published in 2015 in Great Britain by
Barrington Stoke Ltd
18 Walker Street, Edinburgh, EH3 7LP

www.barringtonstoke.co.uk

Text © 2015 Jo Cotterill
Illustrations © 2015 Jen Collins

A CIP catalogue record for this book is available from the British Library upon request

ISBN: 978-1-78112-449-9

Printed in China by Leo

Contents

Chapter 1
The Best So Far

There was so much clapping! Would it ever end?

The ten members of Burford School Glee Club took another bow. Mel had a big smile on her face. She loved being on stage with the Club. And this had been their best show so far!

As they came off stage, the members of
Glee Club were buzzing. Ms Okoro gave them
all high fives.

"You did me proud," she said. "All that practice paid off. Well done, everyone."

"That was awesome!" Dom said. He did some body-popping and moon-walked across the room.

Cal flicked his floppy blond hair out of his eyes and slapped Dom on the back. "Cool move!" he said.

Mel hugged Jools. "You were amazing." she said.

Jools hugged her back. "Thanks, babe. I wasn't sure about that top D. Did I hit it OK?"

Mel laughed. "Of course you did. Every time!"

Jools was the best singer in Glee Club. She was stunning and her voice was really powerful. She'd got to the 2nd round of 'Britain's Got Talent' last year.

"Only six weeks till the big night," Jools said.

"Bring it on!" everyone shouted. "We're going to thrash Norton High!"

"Glee Club for ever!" Mel shouted. She punched her fist in the air.

At the end of term, Glee Club was going to compete against all the other schools in the area. Last year, Norton High had beaten them. This year, Mel was *sure* they were in with a chance.

But just a week later a notice went up on the wall.

"Glee Club Cancelled," the notice said.

Chapter 2
A New Music Director

Mel gasped. "Cancelled?" she said. "It can't be! Jools, have you seen this?"

"No way," Jools said. "What's going on?"

Cal stopped to look. "Oh yeah," he said. "Ms Okoro's ill. Didn't you know?"

"Ill?" Mel said. "What's wrong with her?"

"I don't know," Cal said. "But she's in hospital. Miss Wilson said she won't be back this term."

"Oh no!" Mel felt her eyes fill with tears. "Poor Ms Okoro. That's awful."

"She was the reason Glee Club started," Jools said. "She's a fantastic teacher." Jools looked like she was going to cry too.

"She won't be back before the competition," Mel said, as she wiped her eyes. "We can't enter now."

"So Norton High will win again," said Jools. "That totally sucks."

"I wish we could still go," Mel said. "Even if Ms Okoro can't be there."

Jools shook her head. "But how? Who'd teach us the songs?"

Cal looked at Mel. "You could do it," he said.

"Of course!" Jools gasped. "You'd be great, Mel."

"Oh, I don't think I could ..." Mel said. She bit her lip. "Could I?"

"People listen to you," Cal said. "You write songs and you can do harmonies. You're brilliant at music. And you always help out at practice." He flicked his hair out of his eyes and cleared his throat.

Jools turned to Mel. "Say you will!" she begged. "Oh please, Mel. You have to help us beat Norton High. Please say you'll be the

new music director of Glee Club!"

Chapter 3
"Yes, Miss!"

Of course Mel said yes. She loved Glee Club. And she liked the idea of being a music director. Plus, they owed it to Ms Okoro.

The other nine members of the club were all there when Mel arrived for practice.

Mel felt all wobbly. What if no one listened to her? What if they didn't like the song she'd chosen?

Jools smiled at Mel. "You can do it," she whispered, and she gave her a thumbs-up.

"Shut up, you lot!" Dom shouted. "Miss Gold wants to start."

Mel felt even more wobbly. "Don't call me that," she said. "Just call me Mel, like normal."

Some of the others didn't look very impressed. Ms Okoro was a hard act to follow. Mel knew she had to get everyone on side.

"Here's the song," she said, as she handed out sheets of paper. "I've written some harmonies. And I've got the music on my phone."

"Great song," Cal said, as he looked at his sheet.

Mel was pleased. "Thanks, Cal. Shall we give it a go?"

After a few false starts, they sang it all the way through.

"It's amazing, Mel," Jools said. "Well done, babe."

"Thanks, but it still needs work," said Mel.
"Can we try the top line again?" She made
them sing it over and over again.

After the 10th or 11th time, Mel smiled. "That's really good now," she said.

The others looked happy too. "You did a good job on the harmonies," Dom said. "And you're a fantastic teacher."

"Are we all agreed then?" Cal asked. "Mel will train us for the competition, yeah?"

Everyone nodded.

"Totally," Jools said. "She's awesome!"

Mel felt proud of herself. "We've not got long," she reminded them. "So we've got to work really hard."

Cal did a salute like a soldier. "Yes, Miss!" he said with a grin.

Chapter 4
A Secret Crush

The bell had rung for the end of school, but Mel was in the practice room, playing chords on the piano.

Dom knocked on the door. "Can I talk to you?" he asked.

Mel sat back. "Sure, come in," she said. "I'm glad you're here. I need an excuse to stop. This song is doing my head in."

"Oh?" Dom said. "A break will do you good, then." He grabbed a chair and sat next to her. "Look, it's about Jools."

"Jools? What about her?"

"Well ..." Dom went a bit red. He looked at the floor, then at the window. "It's just ..."

"What?" Mel asked.

"I like her," Dom said. "You know."

Mel's mouth dropped open. "Wow! You fancy Jools? I never knew!"

"Ssh!" Dom said. "Don't tell everyone."

"But ... but this is great!" Mel was grinning now. "You'd make a brilliant couple."

"Do you think so?" Dom was loud and confident most of the time, but right now he looked nervous. "Does she like me then?"

Mel took a moment to think. "I don't know," she said. "She hasn't said anything to me."

"Oh," Dom said. "Maybe ... maybe it's not a good idea."

Mel felt sorry for him – he looked so sad. "No, it is a good idea," she said. "Do you want me to ask her for you?"

"Yeah, but won't she think I'm chicken?" Dom asked.

"Leave it to me," Mel said. "I can handle it." She leaned forward and gave him a big hug. Dom hugged her back. He looked more cheerful now.

"Thanks, Mel," he said. "You're the best."

Mel looked up and saw Cal at the door. He had a look of shock on his face. Then he turned and walked off.

Mel was puzzled. What was that all about?

Chapter 5
Such a Mess

There was only a week to go before the competition.

"You all sound amazing now," Mel told the others. "And the dance moves are looking good too. Great work on those, Dom."

"We're going to smash the competition!"
Dom said, and he punched the air.

Jools grinned. "We need to win, not kill them."

"That's all for now," Mel said. "Same time tomorrow, everyone."

Dom gave her a look as he went out of the door and Mel nodded. She hadn't had a chance to talk to Jools yet, but now was the perfect time.

"Can we go over that last bit again?" Jools asked her. "Only I still don't think I'm doing it right."

"You're fine," Mel said. "It sounds great. We can practise together later if you want, but listen ... I need to ask you something. It's about Dom."

"What about him?" Jools asked.

"Do you ... er ... do you like him?" Mel asked. "Fancy him, I mean?"

Jools's skin glowed with embarrassment. "Why are you asking?"

"He's such a nice guy," Mel said. "He's funny and he's great at the dance stuff. Don't you think?"

"It sounds more like *you* fancy him," Jools said.

"No, it's not that at all," Mel said. "Jools ..."

"Look," said Jools. "If you like Dom, you should go out with him." She picked up her bag. She was frowning now. "You don't have to ask *me* what *you* should do about Dom."

Mel followed her to the door. This was not going at all how she had hoped. "Jools, you don't get it," she said. Her voice shook with panic.

"I get it all right," Jools said in a loud voice. "You fancy Dom. It's fine. Just go out with him, OK?"

Jools opened the door. Cal was standing on the other side.

"Oh – hi, Cal," she said.

"Hi," Cal said, but he looked at Mel, not Jools. "I came to ask Mel something. But it can wait."

"As long as you weren't going to ask her out," Jools said. "She's already taken." And with that, she walked off.

Mel's face felt like it was on fire. "Hi," she said, but her voice came out like a squeak.

Cal opened his mouth and shut it again.
His face was red, too. He frowned at her,
then walked away without another word.

Mel put her hands over her eyes. She
wanted to say "I'm not taken!" – but it was
too late. Now both Jools and Cal would think
she fancied Dom. This was such a mess!

Chapter 6
Practice Makes Perfect

Dom turned up early for the next rehearsal.

"What did Jools say?" he asked Mel. "Did you speak to her? Will she go out with me?"

Mel didn't know how to tell him.

"It sort of went wrong," she said. "Now she thinks I fancy you. And she told *me* to go out with you."

"What?" Dom looked gutted. "Sorry, Mel. I like you and everything, but ..."

Mel jumped in. "No, it's OK," she said. "I don't fancy you either. You should totally go out with Jools. But I messed everything up. Now I don't know how she feels. She got the wrong end of the stick. And now she's mad at me."

"I shouldn't have said anything," Dom said. "Forget it, Mel."

Mel wanted to say more, but the others had arrived. She shook her head. It was no good trying to sort this mess out now. There was work to be done.

It was a hard rehearsal. Mel made the group do their two songs over and over again.

"My legs are killing me," Kyra moaned. She took off her glasses and cleaned them on her top.

"Yeah, and my throat hurts," Billy said.

Mel looked at him in alarm. He was the best boy singer they had. "Your throat hurts?" she asked.

"Yeah. I need to rest it," Billy said. "Or I won't have a voice left at this rate."

Mel bit her lip. "All right. We'll stop. But it isn't quite perfect yet. Tally, you need to be careful in the first verse. You're singing a bit flat. And Lucy, you keep going right instead of left in the dance break."

"There's still one rehearsal to go," Jools said. Her voice was sharp. "Stop fussing, Mel."

Jools, Dom and Cal all left without saying goodbye. Mel felt like crying. All this hard work – and now her friends weren't talking to her. What was the matter with Jools? Jools normally backed Mel up.

Mel closed her eyes and crossed her fingers. The competition was what mattered. They had to beat Norton High. The other stuff would just have to wait.

But that night, Mel couldn't sleep. She kept thinking about Cal and his face when

Jools told him Mel fancied Dom. Cal was the nicest boy she knew. Did he think of her as more than a friend? And had she blown her chance to find out?

Chapter 7
Go For It

It was the day of the competition.

Mel was so nervous that she felt sick. The last rehearsal had not gone well. Billy still had a sore throat, and Lucy kept getting her dance moves wrong.

At the end of school, the Glee Club members all got on a minibus. Mel was glad when Jools sat next to her. "Hi, Jools!" she said.

But Jools just shook her head.

"What is it?" Mel asked.

Jools opened her mouth. "Voice," she whispered. "Gone. Lost my voice."

Mel's mouth fell open. "You've lost your voice? But ... but, Jools!" Jools sang solo on the first song. What were they going to do?

Dom leaned over from the seat in front. "What's going on?" he asked.

Mel gripped the seat. "It's a disaster," she said. "Jools can't sing!"

Everyone gasped.

"I'm so sorry," Jools croaked. "It was OK this morning."

"It's not your fault," Dom said. He put a hand on her arm. "Don't blame yourself."

Jools had tears in her eyes. "I don't want to let everyone down."

Mel was trying to think. "Is there someone else who can sing your part?" she asked.

There was silence.

"The only one who knows all the parts ..." Cal said in a soft voice, "is you."

"Me?" Mel said with a gulp. "But … but I don't sing solo."

"But you have a great voice," Dom said. "We know you do. You sing all the time in rehearsals."

Jools was nodding hard. "Yes, yes," she whispered. "You can do it, Mel!"

Mel felt dizzy. Could she really do it? She knew the part, but she'd never sung solo before. It would be in front of everyone – and in the competition against Norton High!

But then she looked at Cal. He was smiling at her.

"Go for it, Mel," Cal said. "We believe in you."

And the smile on his face made Mel feel like she could do anything.

Chapter 8
And the Winners Are

The Glee Club competition was under way.

Mel and her friends sat and watched the other schools. They were all very good. Then Norton High came onto the stage. Their songs were way better than anyone else's. They looked like the clear winners.

Mel and Jools looked at each other. Mel knew what Jools was thinking. There was no way they could beat Norton High.

Jools gripped Mel's hand. "Knock them dead," she whispered.

It was time. Mel and the members of Glee Club took their places on the stage. Out in the crowd, Jools gave a big thumbs-up.

The music started. Mel opened her mouth – and sang. To her surprise, her voice didn't shake and her legs didn't wobble. And the rest of the group sang and danced with her, and it was amazing! Then the second song began, and Billy forgot his sore throat and sang like he'd never sung before. And Lucy got her dance steps right, and Tally sang in tune – and then it was all over!

Mel had a big smile on her face. They'd done it! Maybe they weren't as good as Norton High, but they'd done a great job.

The presenter asked all the school clubs to come back onto the stage. "The judges have made up their minds," she said. "And the winners are ..."

Mel held her breath.

"Burford Glee Club!"

"Oh my God," Mel gasped. "We won!"

"Melody Gold, the director," the presenter
said. She came over with a big silver cup.
"Well done!"

Mel didn't think she could be any happier. But then she saw Dom jump off the stage and run to Jools. He said something to her, and she gazed at him. And then she threw her arms around his neck and kissed him!

Mel turned to Cal. "Did you see that?" she asked.

Cal was looking the other way. "Look who's over there," he said.

Ms Okoro was at the back of the hall, waving and cheering as hard as anyone else. Mel shouted and waved back and held up the silver cup. "Look!" she called. "We did it!"

Ms Okoro gave Mel a thumbs-up and a big smile, as if to say, "I knew you could!"

Mel turned to Cal. "This cup is yours really. It was you who said I should run Glee Club. I didn't know I could do it."

Cal grinned. "OK, I'll share it with you," he said. "But tell me something. Are you going out with Dom?"

"Of course not," Mel said. "He fancies Jools – look!" She pointed to where Dom and Jools were still snogging.

"Ohhh!" Cal said. "That's made me very happy. So you're not taken then?"

"Taken?" Mel grinned. "No. I'm not taken. Did you have someone in mind for me?"

"Yeah." Cal looked into her eyes. "Yeah, I did, in fact."

"You know we're still on stage, right?" Mel said. "Everyone can see us."

Cal took a step closer. "So?" he said. And he kissed her.

Our books are tested
for children and young people by
children and young people.

Thanks to everyone who consulted on
a manuscript for their time and effort in
helping us to make our books better
for our readers.